What C

Contents	Page

written by Pam Holden

I will be a mountaineer
when I am big.

mountaineers

Then I can climb to the top of mountains.

I will be a scientist when I grow up.

I will be a farmer when I am big.
Then I can look after all my animals.

6

farmer

I will be an explorer
when I grow up.

explorer

I will go into forests and deserts.

I will be an astronaut when I am big.

I will fly into space and go to the moon.

I will be a dancer when I grow up.

dancers

Then I can dance on the stage.

I will be a musician
when I am big.

musician

I will play the piano and write songs.

artist

I will be an artist.
Then I will paint a
picture of you!

16